Library and Archives Canada Cataloguing in Publication

Title: The most beautiful thing I have ever seen / written by Nadia Devi Umadat ; illustrated by Christine Wei.
Names: Umadat, Nadia Devi, author. | Wei, Christine, illustrator.
Identifiers: Canadiana (print) 20220464790 | Canadiana (ebook) 20220464820 | ISBN 9781772603149 (hardcover) | ISBN 9781772603156 (EPUB) | ISBN 9781772603309 (Kindle)
Classification: LCC PS8641.M33 M67 2023 | DDC jC813/.6—dc23

Printed and bound in Canada

Second Story Press gratefully acknowledges the support of the Ontario Arts Council and the Canada Council for the Arts for our publishing program. We acknowledge the financial support of the Government of Canada through the Canada Book Fund.

Published by
Second Story Press
20 Maud Street, Suite 401
Toronto, Ontario, Canada
M5V 2M5
www.secondstorypress.ca

Nadia Devi Umadat is a Canadian social worker. She was born in Toronto, though her family is originally from Guyana. For several years she supported newcomer and refugee families taking their first steps toward making Canada their home. *The Most Beautiful Thing I Have Ever Seen* is inspired by her adventures with Syrian children. When Nadia was in school, she got in trouble all the time for talking too much. Now she tries to write her thoughts down when she can. She loves reading, being a tourist, and searching for beautiful things!

Christine Wei is a Taiwanese artist living on the unceded territories of the Musqueam, Squamish, and Tsleil-Waututh Nations in Vancouver, BC. She graduated from Emily Carr University of Art and Design with a Bachelor of Fine Arts and major in illustration. Christine's work often draws inspiration from sentiment, life stories, and nature-inspired mark-makings. She loves creating art with a variety of mediums to convey relatable narratives in dynamic perspectives.

To my friends at CCVT with lots of love and appreciation. And to Noah, my bestie.
—N.D.U.

For the ones who dream of kinder worlds.
—C.W.

The Most Beautiful Thing I Have Ever Seen

Written by Nadia Devi Umadat

Illustrated by Christine Wei

Second Story Press

My first home was in a hot,
faraway place.
I always had other children to play
with besides my bossy sister.
We had lots of fun and plenty of food.

But one day, the parties stopped.
We had to stay inside because bad
things were happening all around us.
There were loud noises everywhere,
and they made Mama cry.
That was the saddest thing
I had ever seen.

One night, Mama woke us and told us to be very quiet.
She bundled us outside to a waiting van.
Some of our neighbors were already inside.
I tried to stay awake, but I was so tired.

In the morning light, I saw many
destroyed buildings all around us.
We were taken to a tiny, crowded room.
Everyone was serious all of the time.

Then, one day, Mama became very excited.
She packed what we had left in a suitcase.
"We are going to live in a new home far away,"
she said.
I didn't know where that was.
"I don't want to go," I told her.
"You can stay here if you want, but I'm going,"
said my bossy sister.
She might have been joking, but I wasn't so sure.

A stranger drove us to
the airport.

We stood in a line, and they X-rayed our suitcase.
There were thousands of people heading in every direction.
We boarded a huge, shiny airplane.

Mama let me have the window seat.
Puffy white clouds, some shaped like animals, glided
with us in the sky.
It was the most amazing thing I had ever seen.

I drifted along with the clouds until I fell asleep.
In the morning, Mama gently woke me.
Our plane had landed.
We gathered our belongings and left through the exit.
And there stood Aunty, waiting for us.

"Oh, how I've missed you," she
said, holding all three of us close.
Mama's face was wet with tears.
This time I wasn't sad, because
happy crying is nice.

Aunty drove us to our new apartment.
It was small, but larger than the
crowded room we'd stayed in.
The walls were freshly painted pale blue, like the sky.
We had a brand-new fridge and a shiny silver stove.

There was a big double bed and
a smaller single bed.
"Mama gets this one, I get that one, and you
get the floor," said my bossy sister.
I hoped she was joking, but I wasn't so sure.

One day, it was time
for me to start school.
I'd never been to school before.
I was excited but nervous, too.
Aunty walked with me and introduced
me to my teacher.
She smiled and spoke to the class in
words I did not understand.
So many children, so many
eyes stared at me, like I was the
strangest thing they had ever seen.

Later, a siren sounded, as loud as the
noises from our first home.
My classmates got up and left the room.
I didn't know where to hide, so I started to cry.
My teacher showed me how to take deep
breaths and calm down.

Together, we looked through the window and
watched everyone play.
When I told my bossy sister about the siren, she
gave me a look.
"It's called recess. You'll get to like it."

I had English class every morning.
I wasn't alone.
There were lots of other children who were new, too.

I made friends in my class, but learning
English was hard.
Still, day by day, word by word, I
understood more and more.
My family and friends helped me feel safe.
I almost forgot the scary things from before.
Almost.

Aunty told us about our new country's
different seasons.
The days got darker and colder.

We had to wear coats and hats,
mitts and boots.
We looked silly and felt too heavy to move.
But one December morning, shimmery white
powder covered the ground.
Cold and soft, it sparkled in the sun.
It was the most magical thing I had ever seen.

"It's called snow!" my bossy sister said.

We ran outside and caught snowflakes on our tongues.

We made snow
angels and
snowballs.
We laughed till
our sides ached.

We hardly noticed the
cold at all.
Then I slipped and fell
down hard.

My sister helped me
stand and brushed
me off.
"There. You're all
right now," she said.
She wasn't even
joking.

The days grew longer, the snow
melted away, the ground warmed up.
Flowers bloomed on trees and in gardens.
School ended for the summer.
Neighbors invited us to our country's
birthday party in the park.
"How can a country have a birthday party?" I wondered.
"Don't ask," my sister said. "There will be fireworks."
I had never seen fireworks before.
Everyone seemed excited, but especially Mama.

I think if you've been really afraid, a bit of
fear stays with you even when you're safe.
The sky got darker, and the lights shot
up over our heads.
Suddenly there was a loud *Kaboom!*
I jumped up and looked around.
My bossy sister wasn't far away, but her
eyes were so wide. She couldn't move.
Like me, she remembered the terrible
noises from our first home.
I moved closer and showed her how to
take deep breaths and calm down.

Slowly, we began to feel better.
We were safe in the park together with
Mama, Aunty, and our friends.
The fireworks were loud but they
were also dazzling.
My bossy sister slid her hand into mine.
I squeezed her fingers and felt warm, even
in the cool night air.
"Don't stand next to me," she whispered.
She was definitely joking.

We are now home.
We have seen all the seasons
and many snowfalls.
This morning, I put on my very best clothes.
We are in a big government building for
a special ceremony.
Today, we become citizens.
A judge asks us to take an oath.
My mama, my bossy sister, and I are with many
people of every shape, size, and color.

The judge makes a speech, and
I understand almost all of it.
"Welcome," she says, smiling at everyone.
The whole group claps and
cheers and hugs each other.
Aunty and Mama cry happy tears. I wipe
away a few of my own.
My bossy sister says, "Don't embarrass me,"
and gives me one of her tissues.
She uses the other one.
It is the most beautiful thing I have ever seen.